Sweet Love of Mine

BRIDES
OF
ADORATION

Bestselling Author
JOSEPHINE BLAKE

Contact the author via her website at:
www.awordfromjosephineblake.com

Thank you for purchasing *Sweet Love of Mine* by
Josephine Blake. Enjoy!

"For the world, when seen through a little girl's eyes greatly resembles Paradise."
-Anonymous-

CHAPTER ONE

"I think," said Mrs. Cook, "that soup might be best." The three women of the Cook household stood around the large oak-wood table in their farmhouse kitchen, laughing and joking as they scrubbed potatoes with their sleeves rolled up. The men of the household were due home in a handful of hours—they'd been baling hay all day, and were likely to be as hungry as wolves.

"On such a hot day?" Abigail said dubiously. Her mother's potato soup was normally a treat—smooth, velvety, and rich with cream, with just a sprinkle of cracked pepper on top. She liked nothing better than a hot bowl on those chilled winter evenings when the wind managed to force its way through the worn floorboards and walls. Despite her father's best efforts to stopper the cracks in the weeks before the chills came, the house was often drafty and cold in the winter.

In the heat of a summer that stubbornly refused to leave,

however, Abigail could not think of anything that she might want to eat less.

She glanced over at her older sister, Hannah. The girl's face was soft and peaceful, despite being flushed from the heat, and she knew instantly that her sister must have recently received another letter from her fiancé, Jonathan Stone. Whenever she did, nothing could rouse her from this dreamy state for inveritable hours afterward. There would be no help from her.

"Summer has seemed to linger, hasn't it?" Her mother sighed and swirled one of the potatoes around in the brackish water. "Perhaps," she said, thoughtfully, "we could slice them, pan-fry them with salted pork, and have some tomatoes in cream, and fresh greens—"

As she spoke, Abigail's mind began to wander. She knew her mother would come up with something delicious for supper after a hard day's work—she always did. However, her mother's defaulting to potatoes—they had had them thrice already, and it was only Thursday—meant that provisions were low.

She had heard murmurings behind her parent's closed bedroom door. Harvest had not been the best this year. There had been grasshoppers, and weevils, and a heavy, rainy spring that had caused rot. First the oats, then the corn, and finally the wheat had not been viable—and not only was Mr. Cook's livelihood threatened, so was their food supply for the winter.

Abigail knew they were in no real danger; her ever-frugal father saved much every year for events such as these. Still, a new threshing machine and collected expenses from previous weeks would ensure this winter would be a lean one at best.

"Turned dresses and hand-me-down shoes," Abigail muttered under her breath, then she immediately felt guilty. It was not her parent's fault that the grasslands of Oregon had chosen to be cruel this year.

It's not as if you're doing anything to help. At least Hannah was bringing home money to her mother and father every week from her job as a hostess at the West Hotel, despite the fact that Abigail knew her older sister was hoping to save for her imminent wedding to Jonathan Stone. Her brothers did odd jobs as well, hiring themselves out to other farms in the area once the Cook harvest had been brought in. Her mother, as she had always done at various times of hardship, took laundry in from Neil Lavan's practice. Everybody did their part.

Everybody, Abigail thought despondently, *but me.*

It was not as though she had not attempted to find something—she had. Proper jobs for girls included cleaning, as Hannah had, dressmaking, cooking, teaching, laundry. Abigail was an appalling tailor, an even worse cook, and her tiny frame was badly suited to emptying and washing straw-ticks and heavy quilts, as her mother did. Teaching was out; Adoration's tiny school was already fully staffed.

*But I am not **completely** useless*, she told herself defiantly, and she bit the inside of her cheek. She must find some way to help. This was beginning to stretch beyond her given duty as a daughter, it was becoming a matter of pride.

None of the stress of the hours before was showing on Mrs. Cook's face when the family all sat down to supper; there was laughter, teasing, and fresh-scrubbed faces, all bright and happy around the enormous farm table. The meal, of course, was delicious. Platters of pan-fried potatoes, seasoned to perfection, and breaded salt pork were passed around on platters, and there was an enormous pot of simmering greens, drowning in buttery, spicy pot-liquor—the last of the season, probably. There were corn fritters, and to complete the meal, tomatoes and sugar in cream. They ate until they were stuffed full and traded jokes, stories, and advice. Abigail's heart swelled with love for her family as she gazed around the table. *There will never be,* she thought, *a nicer bunch of folks anywhere.* She counted her blessings in each of her siblings' smiles, and in the affectionate arm her father draped over her mother's shoulders.

"No one," her father declared, pushing back his plate. "Not a single one of you girls is as pretty as your mother."

They laughed, and Mrs. Cook snorted, though her face was flushed with pleasure. "A full belly will make your father say anything," she responded tartly, and that set them off again.

"I've a funny story to tell you," he said, scratching his beard with every indication of contentment. Abigail knew he would have loosened his belt a few notches were their mother not at the table to hiss "Elijah—!" at him.

"What is it, Papa?" This was Hannah, who had deigned to drift out of the clouds by dinnertime.

"Today, while in town off-loading hay," he chuckled. "Do you all know that young man with a ranch just south of ours, other side of the river? The cattle-farmer?"

They nodded. He was not someone Abigail had been formally introduced to, though she had interacted with him in the past, at town events, and the like. She hunted for a memory and it brought up the image of a man with reasonably broad shoulders, of medium height, with fair hair bleached white from the sun. The mental apparition vanished with her father's booming voice. "He rode," he said, "past William's shop this morning, in that light trap of his, with a baby on the front seat."

His wife gaped. "A baby?"

Her father grinned. "A baby." He began to chuckle. "The man was sweating as hard as a horse-thief. He was driving that cart as gently as a man can drive, cursing every pebble and loose stone along the way, and the poor mite in her basket was just wailing away."

"Oh, dear!"

Mr. Cook wiped his eyes. "I know. Every man on the street stopped to stare. He pulled up to the parson's house and started banging the door, picked up the wee mite as if she were a live rattlesnake,. 'Help,' he hollered, 'It's a matter of life and death!'"

Looking around at his spellbound audience he continued. "The parson's wife answers, and he just starts babbling. Says he can't get her to eat. He's tried everything—meat, and potatoes, and rice, and pork—"

"For a baby?" Mrs. Cook gasped.

"That was when most of the street started to laugh."

Abigail's brothers guffawed, but they were quiet when their mother shot them a look. "I think it's dreadful," his wife said disapprovingly. "Poor man. Why in heaven's name does he have the care of a child, Elijah? He's not married?"

"His brother and his wife passed away rather sudden-like, left the little girl to him."

"Oh, Elijah," her mother said with compassion, and Abigail's father actually looked fairly ashamed of himself.

"It's a hard thing," he said, clearing his throat.

"What in heaven's name is that bachelor going to do with a baby?"

He shrugged. "I'm not sure. The parson's wife rode off with him. I suppose she'll get them settled, show him what to do."

Her mother made no further comment, compressing her lips.

When the women cleared the table after dinner, she reached out and touched Abigail's arm. "Pack a basket of provisions," she said, "and take it to young James Taylor. Things a baby would need—milk, cream, eggs, soft bread. If Mrs. Grant is indeed there with him she'll show him what to feed the baby, but..." her voice trailed off as she shook her head. "Lost his brother, and his sister in law, too. Such a terrible shame."

A half hour later, the farmhouse kitchen and dining room were spotless, and Abigail was headed towards James Taylor's ranch, hauling the heavy basket her mother had packed with both hands.

If little Beth made that positively awful sound once more, James thought in despair, he might actually lose his mind.

He was pacing back and forth in the main hallway of his ranch. It was the longest stretch in his home, and he'd walked it at least ten hundred times once Beth had started screaming. She'd waited, naturally, until the parson's wife had left, leaving him with the cheery admonition to "just relax, it will all become more natural!" and a wave.

It had not become more natural, not at all, and it wasn't five minutes after the parson's wife had disappeared over the hill that Beth's bottom lip had started trembling. Her round cheeks flushed, and her eyes—already enormous and blue, like his brother's had been— began filling with tears.

"Don't, child," he'd murmured, but it was useless—his little niece, clearly as uncertain about his ability to parent as he was, opened her pink mouth and began to wail. He might start to weep himself, if she didn't stop.

He sighed, lifting the chubby infant to his left shoulder as Mrs. Grant had taught him to do. The little girl had every reason to cry; she'd been in the world for only a year, lost both parents to scarlet fever in the space of a month, and was now subject to the tender mercies of her only living relative; a grossly incompetent, bachelor uncle.

He would cry too in such a situation, he thought. He'd had no time to process his brother's death, no time at all to mourn, and his niece had every reason to sob at him, having no understanding of where her mother and father had gone and why they could not return to her.

James began gently bouncing the girl up and down, up and down—she screamed all the more. What did she want? She'd been fed, he felt no wetness through her linens. Perhaps she wanted fresh air—was fresh air good for babies, or not? The parson's wife had told him, although James could not remember his own name at this point, let alone all the scattered bits of advise she'd thrown at him throughout the course of the day.

Beth was hollering so loud that James nearly missed the gentle tapping at his door. Whoever it was hesitated and then tapped again, a little louder.

"I'm coming!" He called over Beth's shrieks. He hurried to the door and threw it open, gazing in some haphazard manner at the young woman that stood on the front step. She was short enough to be a child, but her long skirts and slim curves spoke otherwise. Her dark blonde hair was pulled back into a simple braid, and she held a basket so large she had to carry it with both hands.

"Hello," she said, a little shyly, but her eyes flickered curiously to the screaming baby on his shoulder. James shifted her about and, to his surprise, when Beth saw the little woman she stopped short as if shocked, and took a deep, shuddering breath.

His mind seemed to relax. fractionally, at the new lack of bellowing beside his ear. Self-conscious, James took a step back.

"I'm Abigail," the woman said simply, then she held out the basket. "My mother sent me over with some provisions for your niece, and I—"

"Come in," he said quickly. He saw surprise register in her eyes, but she lifted her narrow chin and stepped over the landing. The moment they were back in the shadowy darkness of the ranch house, Beth began to scream, again. Frustrated, James took the basket from Abigail, dumping the baby into her arms at the same time. "Do something!"

"Me?" Abigail exclaimed. She trotted after him, jiggling Beth up and down in the same way he had just moments ago. The baby was equally unimpressed.

"She won't stop."

"And I'm supposed to know how to help her?"

"You're a woman, aren't you?" James shot back, running his free hand through his frazzled hair. He emptied the contents of the basket out on the kitchen table with little ceremony, glancing at her.

Abigail sputtered. "I don't have any children!"

"One would hope not." He rummaged frantically. There was a custard pie, a jar of milk, rice pudding...

Abigail huffed. "You'll spoil everything there! Here, let me—" and she lifted Beth back into his arms.

"There's a good girl," she cooed, and turned round. "Where are the spoons?"

"She isn't hungry, the parson's wife just fed her."

"You never can be sure with babies," Abigail said gravely.

He was willing to try anything.

Rice pudding was pushed away at once, with the little girl's face wrinkling in abject disgust. She took one bite of custard and sobbed. When mashed potatoes with cream were offered, the little girl shoved the entire bowl to the floor, screaming at the top of her lungs now.

"You see?" James sighed, bending to retrieve the bowl and going in search of a damp cloth.

"Diaper?" Abigail asked. A bit of hair had escaped her braid and was curling around her cheeks in the damp heat.

"I checked. She was freshened up less than an hour ago."

"Let's check." Abigail laid the little girl on the dining-room table, then awkwardly began to unwind the layers of clean white muslin the parson's wife had wrapped her in.

When the air hit her bare skin, Beth stopped thrashing, and her legs fell limply to the table. Her bottom lip puckered pathetically.

James' first reaction was relief, but it was immediately eclipsed by an onslaught of panic. The little girl's tummy, thighs and knees were covered with mottled red-and-pink patches.

"Prickly heat," Abigail said softly. This, she knew plenty about, having spent many a summer miserable, damp and itchy in her long-sleeved dresses. "I've spent many a day in my room because I didn't want to put clothes on."

As soon as the statement was out of her mouth she realized how horribly indelicate it was and blushed rosy red. However, James merely looked at her curiously, and the planes of his deeply tanned face settled into a smile that quite transformed it.

"You're definitely not as lucky as your brothers were— we generally just jump in the creek."

"Jay-bird naked," Abigail said with a laugh, which was of course not at all the thing to say, either. However, there was something about this James Taylor that overcame her reticence quickly. Perhaps it was the fact that she'd seen him in such a vulnerable position, or the fact that he clearly cared for his little niece so very much. He could have left her in an orphanage, or with a relative, and yet, he'd insisted on doing what he was wholly unsuited for.

"Yes," he said, and gave her a long, curious look.

Abigail cleared her throat. "I can treat this," she said briskly. "Or at least make her a little more comfortable, if you'll let me?"

"I'd be grateful. What do you need?"

"A wash-tub, the one you use for dishes is fine. Nothing too big. A bucket of cool well-water, and the lightest dress she has..."

As he raced about, collecting the things, Abigail undressed Beth. The little girl grew happier with the removal of each layer of clothing and by the time Abigail lowered her carefully into the tub of water, Beth was laughing happily.

"It cools her body down, and allows the skin to settle," Abigail explained.

"I see."

"If she's still sweaty at bedtime, you can dip a cloth in cool water and sponge her off that way." He'd be by himself tonight with the baby, Abigail realized, and her heart went out to him. Silence descended on James' small kitchen; it was broken only by the sound of Beth's cooing and her fat little hands slapping on the water. After a moment Abigail cleared her throat.

"She doesn't look much like you," she said, chucking the baby's dimpled chin, and making her laugh. The saucer-like eyes and tufts of soft hair were distinct, but looked little like James.

"She favors her ma."

"Her mother must have been beautiful."

"That she was."

Abigail was almost sorry she had mentioned it; she could see him swallowing, hard. "I'm so very sorry for your loss, Mr. Taylor," she said simply.

Silence fell for another moment; then, he cleared his throat.

"James," he said. "I thank you."

Abigail focused back on the little girl in front of her, smiling again. She flicked her braid over her shoulder; Beth was doing her best to drag it into the water. The pair chuckled.

"You must dine with me before you go home," he invited. "Your mother has sent over so much."

"That's for the baby, really."

"Then you must allow me to empty my own larder," he said. His tone was curiously formal, but his eyes were kind. Good breeding, she remembered her mother saying, and stood a little straighter herself.. "You don't know how indebted I am to you."

"I'd do anything for this sweet girl," Abigail said lightly. She leaned forward to kiss Beth's nose; the girl laughed and wrapped her chubby arms around Abigail's neck, splashing them all soundly. James smiled, but he wasn't really looking at her; his eyes were focused somewhere very far away, beyond the room, even.

"I just can't help but think," he said in a rough, uneven tone— "and this is the worst of it. She hasn't a clue her parents are dead."

It was as if all of the air went out of the room. Sadness gripped Abigail's heart, and she suddenly wished that it would not be improper for her to reach out and touch him, too. He just looked so absolutely gutted—and she realized in that instant that he'd lost a brother and a sister in this, too.

"She has you," Abigail said firmly. Her desire to comfort him was overcoming the reservations she'd normally have with a stranger, and she continued rapidly. "She hasn't a mother and father, but she has an uncle that cared enough not to leave her to the care of strangers, but brought her home in his wagon without a minute's hesitation, and is doing his best to learn how to care for her, and—"

James coughed, and she saw his eyes were glistening.

"Pardon," was all he said, and he hurried from the room, leaving Abigail with a suspicious dampness in her own eyes, and the chubby little girl's arms still wrapped tightly around her neck.

Abigail sighed and smiled softly as Beth squashed her cheek against her own, then settled back into the water to splash some more.

Why, James thought, taking a deep, shaky breath in he hallway, had he decided to lose his composure now? He'd been dry-eyed when he received the news, and at the funeral, and when he'd collected the little girl at the parson's home, ignoring the looks of doubt on their faces. Aside from his panic when he'd realized that caring for a baby was very different from rearing a puppy, he'd been just fine—until he was subject to the ministrations of this tiny girl from the Cook farm whose large eyes shone with a kindness that his heart craved, just at that moment.

James coughed again and shook his head. He had no intention of boo-hooing in front of a slip of a girl, no matter how kind she was being to him.

James returned only a minute or two later, holding an enormous square of worn, but clean flannel. It smelled faintly of sunshine, and soap. "I haven't got much by the way of towels," he said without alluding to their previous conversation. Thankfully Abigail did not, either.

"It's fine," Abigail said quietly. She made as if to lift the little girl from the water, but James shook his head.

"May I try?"

"By all means." Abigail stood aside, and James lifted the little girl from the tub, cradling her close to his chest. Beth whined a bit, but before she could say, "No!" Abigail bent and peered into the little girl's face. James felt his chest tighten; the picture was a sweet one, and he doubted anyone with a heart would be unaffected by it.

"This is your uncle, sweet girl. Be nice to him—yes?"

Beth looked at Abigail, then at James, then broke into an enormous smile. They both began to laugh.

When they finished, James dusted the baby with a sweet-smelling powder the parson's wife had brought and helped her awkwardly into her long cambric nightgown; Abigail diapered her, and tied a tiny bonnet over Beth's brown curls.

He liked the way Abigail went about her business; she had a talent for being helpful without making him feel completely incompetent, as the parson's wife had done.

When she looked up, he started, felt his cheeks warm. He

spoke quickly, diffusing the tension in the air.

"How would you like a position here?"

She blinked, and then she smiled.

CHAPTER TWO

When *Abigail returned to the* Cook farm, hair streaming in the wind, she was so breathless that she could hardly speak when she burst into the kitchen. The sun had succumbed to the warm fall night, and she inadvertently allowed several lightening-bugs indoors along with the muggy air.

"Abigail Susan Cook," her mother scolded, but Abigail was far too excited.

"He wants to hire me, hire me, hire me!" she cried, picking up her skirts and dancing about.

Her parents exchanged looks. "Whom?" demanded her mother.

"James Taylor. He asked if I would work for him, and take care of little Beth."

"What?" her mother exclaimed.

"Yes. He will pay me as much as he pays his hired girl. I'll come after breakfast, and leave right before supper—"

"Is that why you took so long to get back? Because he was making you an offer? Abigail Susan," her mother said sternly, and Abigail managed to rein it in a bit.

"No, ma'am. I helped him bathe Beth—"

"Who in heaven's name is Beth?"

"His niece!"

Mrs. Cook lifted her hands helplessly and sank down in the nearest chair. "My land."

"Isn't it wonderful?" Abigail's heart felt as light as froth—so much lighter than it had that morning. "I can help out now—I call it downright Providential."

"I call it unnecessary," her father said, sternly. "While things may be a little strained this season, there is no reason why my daughters need to hire themselves out like threshers."

"Hannah has a job."

"That is different. Hannah took work long before any of this happened, and I didn't like it then either."

"Papa," Abigail whined, but he shook his head.

"It's not proper, Abi. Stuck on a ranch, miles from town, in the company of a single man all day."

"He said that, himself," Abigail said triumphantly. "And I'm to tell you that he has a housekeeper. She is fifty years old and has grown children of her own. He asked me to come work for him because he didn't want to overwork her—she will be there the entire time. And he won't! He works all day."

Her parents exchanged looks again.

"That's probably true," murmured her mother. "A Mrs. Cross. Her husband passed some years back—I know her from the Ladies' Aid Society. She has only pleasant things to say about her employer."

At that, her father's forehead smoothed out a little. "You won't be going there on any days Mrs. Cross is unavailable," he warned.

"No, sir."

"Well—" her father cleared his throat. He still looked unwilling, but not forbidding. "I suppose you have my blessing." He took coffee, then stood and left the room.

Abigail looked at her mother; the older woman smiled, then reached over and patted her daughter's cheek. "He doesn't like the fact," she said simply, "that his daughters feel they have to work."

Oh. Abigail twisted the end of her braid around her fingers. "I don't want Papa to feel bad. I was just tired of feeling so— useless."

"I did not," her mother said emphatically, "give birth to any useless children. You do plenty." She reached out and gave her daughter's hand a squeeze, then a soft smile.

"Mama?"

"Yes, darling?"

"What do I need to know to care for a baby?"

Her mother chuckled. "Why in heaven's name did you take the position if you thought you couldn't do it?"

"Beth liked me," Abigail admitted. "She is a sweet child. And Mr. Taylor..." her voice trailed off.

"Mr. Taylor?" her mother prompted.

"I feel very bad for him," Abigail finished quietly.

Her mother's eyes softened and she nodded.

"It is very tragic, indeed," was all she said, but her fingers on her daughter's cheek were gentle. "Fetch a pencil and some wrapping-paper. You may want to take notes with you."

It was an incredible relief, having help, and after three days of the Cook girl coming early in the morning and leaving after he'd had his supper, James was quite proud of himself for hiring her. Abigail was bright, cheerful, and quick, and Beth adored her. The little girl lit up when she walked through the door, and quieted when she left. With the help of Abigail and the good Widow Cross, James was actually beginning to think that life might someday return to some form of normalcy.

He also had time to grieve. This manifested in hours spent out in the pasture, tending to his herds of cattle, and watching their red backs as they moved across the grassy plain. Their lolling and their bellows had become strangely instrumental in his comfort.

James raised two hundred heads of the fine, fat animals for butchering as well as plowing, and had contracts with businesses both in Adoration and Silverton, providing pounds upon pounds of tough, juicy beef that would end up as steaks and stews and jerky and roasts on tables all over the state. Taylor Beef, he could even brag, was served from sea to shining sea— he had a contract with the railroad, as well.

On Abigail's first day, he took her to the top of Daisy Hill. The location was named for the distinctive white-flowered weeds that grew there determinedly every year, blanketing the grass with a sea of yellow and white. She exclaimed at the hill even from afar, and he dragged off his hat and smiled a little.

"I suppose I should plow over it," he said. "But I can't, somehow. This is how this young lady here got her name," he added, peering down to smile at his niece, whose head was buried in the folds of a wide sunbonnet. She was clinging contentedly to Abigail, and goggling at the flowers.

"But her name is Beth!"

"She's called Daisy, also. My brother said it was nonsensical, but her mother could not be persuaded otherwise." He felt a wistful expression cross his face, then forced a smile immediately. He did not want it to be that sort of trip. Smiling, he indulged Abigail when she urged him to help Beth pick several of the long-stemmed flowers, and they both arrived at the ranch later that day, draped in daisy chains and laughing.

Early in the week, James visited Abigail and Beth from time to time during his workday; and each time, he left feeling contentedly pleased. The young woman was vibrant, lively and full of fun, and occupied little Beth with everything from long walks around the property, to singing, to dancing, to playing with her on a blanket in the grass. All things that he would not have thought of, nor would have had the time to do. That first week, whenever he came home—after the sun had begun to drop in the sky—James was always met with a bright, happy baby girl with a fresh-scrubbed face. She would gurgle and cling to Abigail like a fuzzy squirrel to tree bark.

"She's a natural with her," Mrs. Cross said to him in a private moment, stretching high to whisper in his ear. James grinned.

The older woman did not have to advocate for Abigail, however; the joy on his niece's face said plenty. Having reliable help was a burden off James, himself. He began sleeping better at night, and so did Beth. Her little room was just next to his, and unlike the first two nights, when she'd cried piteously for most of the small hours, she slept soundly now.

By Thursday, James felt well enough about Abigail to spend the entire day away from the ranch, repairing fencing on the North side of his property with Hiram and Silas, two of his many hands. The pair was indistinguishably tall, lanky, and good-natured; they swapped jokes, stories, and bits of news from town as they worked. When the sun rose hot in the sky and the heat became oppressive, the men worked a little slower, taking frequent breaks to sip at the warming water in their jugs.

"It's as hot as blazes out here," Silas said on their third break, and James was inclined to agree. He tipped his hat low over his head, wishing they were nearer the tree line. He turned to survey the area, wondering if there might be a patch of shade cast by a looming oak closer at hand, and then he saw her—Abigail was hurrying toward the men at a terrific pace, lugging something in her right hand.

James leapt up in alarm; his first thought of Beth. However, as he started forward, Abigail gave a cheery wave and he felt himself instantly relax; that was not the greeting of someone who was carrying bad news. She reached them about ten minutes later, quite out of breath; her straw hat was hanging down her back, suspended on a cherry-colored ribbon, and her cheeks were rosy from the heat, her eyes bright.

Behind him, he heard both Silas and Hiram dragging off their hats.

"Abigail, are you all right? Where's Beth?"

"Napping in her basket at Mrs. Cross' feet," she said cheerfully. "I've brought ginger-water for you three. Mrs. Cross just made it and it's very cold." She handed him the large jug she carried and rubbed her arm. "She wanted to bring it, but I thought it too much for her, considering the heat."

"You're very kind." A loud clearing of the throat somewhere behind his left shoulder made James recall his two companions. "This is Silas, and this is Hiram," he added. "I'm sure they're very grateful."

"That we are, Miss," said Hiram, looking at Abigail from head to toe none-too-subtly, and Silas was grinning as well. Despite himself, James felt a rush of irritation. The men clearly thought she was a hired girl, but that was no excuse to gawp at her like a bunch of besotted schoolboys.

Both men came forward.

"Your company's as pleasant a surprise as this cooling drink," said Hiram with a flourish, and James didn't even bother to hide the roll of his eyes. Hiram had an understanding with a Millie Stephens, one town over. He should not be paying gallantries to another young woman, no matter how boring it was out in pasture.

"Thank you," Abigail said with her usual buoyancy; Hiram bowed from the waist, and James had had enough. He took the jug from Abigail. "Thank you, Abigail."

She nodded.

"Perhaps you'd better be getting back, as Beth—"

"Would you like some, Miss?" Hiram said grandly, he took hold of the jug and unstopped it. "I'd be happy to loan my mug if the lady requires a proper glass."

"No, thank you. I'm quite all right. I had plenty before heading out."

Good girl, thought James as he watched her turn from Hiram. "I will leave you now," she said. "There's chicken pie, for supper."

Feeling his ears warm, James nodded stoically as Abigail turned and made her way down the hill, skirts fluttering in the wind. The three men watched in shifty silence until the small figure was fully hidden beneath the shadow of Daisy Hill; then, both of his hired men began to laugh in unison.

"Chicken pie, Taylor?"

"That's why he's left us to our own devices, this week." Silas guffawed.

Hiram reached out, slapping James on the back with a force that clapped his teeth together.

"I'm certain Millie would have appreciated that little display," James said icily, attempting to draw their attention away from Abigail.

"Oh, come off it—I was just playing nice," Hiram chuckled, and then took a swig of the sweet, tangy ginger-water.

"You know, Taylor," said Silas, summoning his sentiments as though from a depth of wisdom—though it was truly coming from marriage not yet six months old, "you were wise to hire her. Give her a month to be settled in, start courting her. You'll be engaged by Michaelmas."

What? James began to sputter, but Hiram was nodding as well.

"Agreed. Cook is a good man, even though his business sense is terrible. She's a pretty thing, and young enough to be useful."

"She's a child!"

The two men exchanged looks.

Well. The more James thought about it—Abigail was clearly no child. He had forced himself to think of Abigail Cook as a mere girl; it had been easier on his conscience, with her long braid and her predisposition to frolic with his niece—to think of her as such.

However, there were many new and interesting thoughts lurking in the shadowy places beneath his good-natured exterior that he did not care to examine... Thoughts that involved Abigail and her warm smile.

In his relaxed and idle moments, James had observed the delicacy of her features. He had noticed, too, her soft rose-and-cream skin, and the fine sprinkling of freckles on her nose. Often, he had caught himself eyeing the way her slender figure moved in and out of the rooms of his home with grace and ease. Any man would have had to have been struck blind not to have seen the fact that Abigail Cook brought light into every space she inhabited.

Hiram and Silas's attentions had brought these thoughts to the surface, and they embarrassed him more than they should have done. Had he not truly noticed Abigail's beauty, he could have chalked up the men's comments to good, old-fashioned ribbing, and likely returned with some jibes of his own. However, he found himself with nothing to say—and his companions, as if sensing his discomfort, quickly moved on to other topics of conversation, though they left him thinking hard.

When James returned to the ranch that evening, muscles aching from the exertion of his first full day at work in a week, he saw Abigail playing on the grass in front of the house with Beth, who was kicking madly and rolling back and forth on a clean sheet. Abigail did not see him approach; it was Beth who saw him first, and she let out a resounding squeal of excitement; Abigail looked over her shoulder, laughed, and then scooped the little girl up, heading to greet him.

"No—no, don't stop on my account, you two are as pretty as a picture," he said lightly, and Abigail's rosy cheeks turned even rosier. James was appalled at the sudden urge to tuck a lock of escaped hair behind one of her soft, shell-like ears; he held out his arms for the baby instead, and Beth readily came to him, lunging determinedly for his hat. The little girl smelled sweetly of soap and clean linen.

"She looks wonderful."

"She was very happy today." Abigail tugged at the end of her braid, a habit of hers that he was beginning to recognize. There were other little things she did that he had begun to take note of; the way she cleared her throat before making a request, the way her skirts swayed when she walked, her laugh that was somehow vigorous and soft at the same time. "I'll take my leave, now?"

He nodded. That morning—before Hiram and Silas had had a go at him—he had been planning to ask her to stay and dine with them, but now something held him back. Perhaps it was the memory of the comments of his hired men. He did not intend to engage Abigail in an entanglement, and in a way, he was grateful for Hiram and Silas's stupidity. It would ensure that he never became too familiar with the girl.

"Good night," she said. Her face was a little worn, and he wondered if she was tired. "I'll see you tomorrow?"

"Why don't you take the day off?" he said, gently. "I'll still pay you. You've worked very hard this week and—" inspiration struck him. "I'll be doing accounts at home, so I'm sure that Mrs. Cross and I can handle Beth, between ourselves."

"Truly?" she asked, hesitantly.

"Truly."

She gave him one of those bright smiles, and it tugged a little at his heart, despite himself.

"Thank you," she said softly; then she came up to him, stood up on her toes, and leaned in. He felt his heart leap up in his chest, then fall as he realized she was kissing Beth's chubby cheek.

"I will see you Monday," she said and was gone, leaving him with the scent of violets and an uncomfortably thudding heart.

When James returned into the house, Beth was already half-asleep on his shoulder, worn out from her exciting day. He went to his study and placed the little girl into the large basket he always left there for her, then he watched her for a few minutes as she fought sleep. When the creases around her eyes softened, and her lids dropped to hide her pretty eyes, James opened a drawer in the massive oak desk he'd had installed years ago.

He pulled out a sheaf of letters, all from his brother. Robert had been a faithful correspondent, much better than James, and in his letters James had a rather detailed history of the last few years of his brother's life.

There were the letters that he had written after he met

Margaret, slowly telling the story of how they fell in love; there was the announcement that she was expecting, and finally, the barely contained joy of a father who has fallen in love with his new child. James had a little of that happiness now. *Just a little*, he thought, looking down at the baby, slumbering peacefully at his feet.

"...I wish very much, brother, that you might one day be as happy as I am now. There is something about witnessing the emergence of new life into a fully realized person that is so tender and lovely; it is simply indescribable. Look away from your ranch for a little bit, James, find you a good wife, and settle down. What you're building will be all the sweeter if you have a partner to join you along the way."

James put down the letter, leaning back in his chair. His heart was heavy, but his thoughts were still with Abigail, and the pretty picture she had made this afternoon, cradling his niece in her arms. He wondered briefly what that might be like, coming home to a pretty face every night, and having someone to talk to about his day besides the stable-boys and Mrs. Cross, then at night—

He shook his head abruptly. There were some places where he had rather his brain not go at this time. He folded the letter carefully, filed it with the others, and slid the packet back into its hiding place. He would keep them carefully for Beth, but for now, they were a comfort to him alone. James stood and stretched, glancing down at his desktop, not really seeing it. A comfort the letters might be, but they always caused him to remember exactly what it was that he had lost, and how lonely the world seemed to be without Jack in it.

CHAPTER THREE

I n the weeks following her employment at the Taylor Ranch, Abigail found herself appreciating Saturdays and Sundays even more. They were the days she spent catching up with her family, hearing the stories of what had happened during the week, and accompanying the family to church on Sunday morning. Being able to pin up her hair and dress in her finest was a lovely change after the busy week, she often told herself—but *James Taylor* also attended these services. A secret, hidden part of Abigail knew she appreciated the opportunity to have him see her in something other than a faded cotton dress and an apron.

This morning, Abigail rose well before the sun, scrambling to do her chores. By the time the grey square of window in she and Hannah's attic bedroom was pale with the light of early morning, Abigail was seeing to her toilette in front of the girls' cracked mirror, which she had propped up on the dressing table. Although she, like everyone else in the house, had had a Saturday-night bath, she sponged herself with violet water, rubbed cream into her hands and cheeks, and carefully unraveled the curl-papers she'd put in the night before. She'd wet them before twisting them up, then wet them again. She'd had to sleep with a rag on her pillow to protect the down inside from dampness. It was worth it, however; when she patiently un-wound each one, she was left with rich, glossy ringlets.

"I hope you primp this much for my wedding," her sister's voice grumbled from beneath the muffling coverlet on their big double bed, and Abigail started, then blushed. She turned to face her sister, who was sitting up and shoving back the sheets, a gentle, teasing half-smile on her face. Each Cook child had one day a week to sleep in where the others took over their chores; Hannah's was Sunday. "I'm impressed at your recent dedication to your looks."

"I've always cared about my looks," Abigail said, defensively.

Her sister chuckled and swung her legs over the side of bed. She did not retract her statement, though, which made Abigail somewhat nervous. She cleared her throat and began working on her hair with hands that seemed to have lost all their dexterity. There was no explanation as to why—Abigail was skilled in this area and usually dressed both her mother and Hannah's silky, hard-to-manage hair.

"I seem to be all thumbs today," she said softly.

Hannah glided over the floorboards, and kissed her cheek.

"Let me help you, although I won't do nearly as good a job as you do." Hannah took up a comb, and Abigail forced herself to relax. Her sister smelled of vanilla and roses; her soft hands were gentle and quick. Abigail felt a little of the tension leave her body; it was nice to be waited on, for once.

"Tell me about Jonathan," she said to her sister. Hannah's big, fair fiancé was traveling through the Western states, and he sent her sister something small from every place he visited; a leather bound book of poetry, a pin for her hair, a square of stained glass in a vibrant color that was neither blue nor green, a box of tiny peppermints. He would give her a ring when he returned, he had promised Hannah, and she had waited faithfully for over a year. Now, as she often did when he was mentioned, she blushed.

"He is fine," she said softly, taking up the comb, and Abigail wondered—for what seemed like the hundredth time—what it must feel like, to love someone to that point of dedication. Hannah's feelings for Jonathan went so much deeper than a pretty dress and an elaborate hairstyle; they were committed to each other in a way Abigail often wondered if she would ever know.

Again she thought of James, then shifted uncomfortably in her chair. The big rancher had made no indication that he thought of her as anything more than Beth's nanny. She wasn't even sure she wanted him to. All she knew at this point was that—well. It would be nice for him to see her looking her best.

Still, she was curious.

As her sister's hands played in her locks; Hannah's reflection in the mirror turned thoughtful. "Do you like James Taylor very much, sister?" she asked abruptly.

Abigail started so violently that Hannah lost her grip on her hair. "I—" she said, confusedly, her eyes going wide. Had she been so obvious?

"He is very handsome, although not so much as Jonathan, of course," her sister laughed.

"I hadn't noticed," mumbled Abigail. Her fingers, desperate for some occupation, found a little sewing-box atop the bureau. She began sorting thread; the blues here, the reds there, the greens in one place, too.

Hannah tilted her head and opened her mouth as if she wanted to say something, then decided against it. "Hand me pins when I ask for them," she said instead, and she began to deftly section, twist and pin her sister's hair. They sat in silence for a moment; then she began speaking softly.

"Jonathan and I," she said, "were friends, first. We had the joy of a shared history, and we will continue to be friends, love affair aside. That will always be our foundation, and will always be there." She hesitated again, then forged forward. "If you are ever to...accept the attentions of a young man...be sure that there is more to your relationship than love, and pretty words. If you cannot be friends, everything else will feel—precarious. Your time together will be defined by an attraction you won't always feel."

"Very well." Abigail could not meet her sister's eyes in the mirror, but she could not discount the validity of her words. "I have no lover, Hannah," she managed.

Hannah pinned the last lock firmly into place—then, she bent and kissed her sister's cheek again.

"I'll leave you to dress," was all she said, and she was gone.

After her conversation with Hannah that morning, Abigail was rather proud of herself for not seeking out her handsome employer that morning in church. *It is impossibly vain*, she told herself sternly, *to use the house of the Lord as an opportunity to show James Taylor what you look like with your hair curled.* Instead, she sought out her friend Clara, a spunky, sweet girl from across town with nut-brown hair and so many freckles on her small face that they quite overshadowed her other features. She exclaimed over Abigail's hair, and the two were in a heated discussion about the newest Youth Companion love-story when Abigail heard someone's throat clear, then a familiar voice.

The two young women turned abruptly. James was standing there. He looked very different in the thin wool suit he wore on Sunday, with its somber waistcoat, tie, and polished shoes rather than boots. Beth was in his arms, dressed in the powder-blue cotton dress that Abigail had sprinkled, ironed, and hung up for her before leaving that Thursday night. The girl squealed excitedly and held out her chubby arms; Abigail took her and laughed aloud, responding to the little girl's babbling with a sound kiss.

"Did you miss me very much?" she exclaimed, and the baby began to giggle. James removed his hat.

"Miss Clara," he said respectfully, and Clara dropped a tiny curtsy.

He turned back to Abigail. "Abigail?"

"Yes?"

"Might you—" he hesitated and looked at Clara.

Clara took the hint. "I'm going to go and tease your brother about his tie, he looks quite grown up in it," she said quickly, and she grinned. She was gone in an instant, and Abigail was left with James, who was shifting his hat nervously from hand to hand. She nuzzled Beth's cheek and waited.

"Would you," he finally said, "take a walk with me this evening? After dinner perhaps?"

Abigail felt her jaw go slack; she recovered quickly.

"I—"

"Unrelated to work, although we certifiably could—" he looked quite ill at ease, and she cut in quickly to alleviate his discomfort.

"That would be nice."

He looked as if he wanted to say something more, and then stopped instead. "Four?" he asked. "I promise I won't keep you for more than an hour—I know your mother tends to worry."

"You know her well."

"She merely does what any responsible mother would. You will be the same, when you have your own children." His lips curved up. "I'll remind you of it."

The words loomed heavy between them, suggestive of something that she had no name for, not now. She fought back a blush—really, there was no need for that—and cleared her throat.

"I would love to walk with you," she said, simply. "Perhaps we could meet at Daisy Hill?" For some reason she could not articulate, she did not want him showing up at the Cook farm, where he would be subject to the scrutiny of her parents and her brothers. It was better to meet him—not exactly in secret, but in a more neutral place. From the look in his eyes, she wondered if he had guessed her thoughts.

"Very well," was all he said, and held out his hands for the baby. "Good day, Abigail."

"Good day."

He was barely gone before Clara came back, brown eyes wide, the skirts of her yellow lawn dress rustling as if as excited as their owner was. "He wants to walk with you this evening?"

"I'm sure it's about Beth, Clara. Perhaps he has some business he wishes to discuss—he is often unavailable for long conversation during the week."

Clara snorted. "Business? On a Sunday? During a stroll in a field of flowers?"

Abigail felt her face grow hot. There had been something in the gentle way he'd looked down at her, Beth in his arms, that was making her look forward to this afternoon's meeting for very different reasons than the ones she'd just proclaimed, despite herself.

Friends, she chided quietly in her head, and she lifted her chin.

"He's just lost his brother and his sister-in-law, and has a very small child as his ward," she said earnestly. "I intend to be his friend as well as his nanny, if I can, but you cannot make such insinuations, Clara. They distress me."

"I'm sorry, then," her friend said softly, and tucked her hand into the crook of Abigail's arm. "You must admit, though," she said, peering into the crowd at James' retreating broad shoulders and tall head, "that he is very handsome. I nearly swooned when he came over here."

Abigail laughed. "Perhaps I should send you to Daisy Hill this afternoon, instead."

Clara shook her head. "And have him turn me away the second he sees me? I think not. 'Miss Clara,'" she drawled in such an accurate imitation of James that Abigail had to smile. "No. He has eyes for you only, my dear."

"Perhaps we should change the subject."

"Perhaps. But, well done, Abby, whether it was purposeful or not. He is, "and here, Clara lowered her voice— "*very* rich. Do not let the farmer's togs fool you. My brother works with John Kent as a clerk in the bank, and John told him he has got thousands just piled away from selling cattle. He is young, handsome and rich, and your father has many children. I am no mercenary, Abby. He came to you, after all. But If I were you,

I'd make sure this walk produced something profitable."

Abigail opened her mouth to retort in disparaging tones, but was cut off when her friend's mother began to call her. Clara slipped her arm from Abigail's, gave her a wink, and then headed off in the direction of her family buggy. Abigail was left standing with her skirts blowing around her ankles, her arms folded protectively over her chest, and her mind whirring silently.

It took Abigail nearly an hour to decide whether she wanted to change out of the cream-colored lawn she had worn to church. Changing would indicate an interest in how she appeared; however, not changing might indicate she thought this meeting of sufficient importance to keep her best dress on. Her mother, to her relief, had little reaction when she told her that she was going for a walk with James Taylor on Daisy Hill.

"Bring him back for supper, if you're out late enough," Mrs. Cook said with studied casualness. "I'd like very much to see that sweet baby girl."

Abigail promised to extend them an invitation, then changed into a fresh dress after much deliberation. She did not want the pale fabric of her Sunday dress to stain in the tall grass of Daisy Hill—with things the way they were, there would be precious few opportunities for new clothes in the upcoming year.

She stood in front of the nails on the wall that served as a closet for her and Hannah; her dresses hung on them, all in a row. There were the two calico dresses she alternated during the week, both of which James had seen plenty of already. There was her second good dress, a grey wool with blue piping—much too hot for this weather. She finally selected the last, a fawn-colored gown with a feathery cream pattern she had inherited from Hannah. She liked the way it brought out the shine in her hair. She dressed quickly and headed out for the Taylor farm.

James stood at the foot of Daisy Hill, still dressed in his suit for church; his arms were empty. She waved, and then hurried over, lifting her skirts to avoid the tall grass.

"Where's Beth?" she said a little breathlessly, and he smiled.

"I left her with Mrs. Cross. She agreed to do a few hours this afternoon in exchange for some time with her sister, this week."

"Oh." So they were to be alone, then. Abigail bit her lip hard to distract from the familiar rush of blood to her cheeks—how much did she blush when she was with him, for goodness' sake? She would have been flustered, but Hannah's soft voice came to her, unbidden, as if her older sister were standing there with her.

Be a friend, first.

At that thought, a smile crossed Abigail's face—a wide, gentle smile that came effortlessly, and he smiled back, a little hesitantly, as if he wasn't sure what he was supposed to do in that kind of social situation. It was somewhat endearing. "Shall we walk, then?" she said, and gestured. James did not try to take her arm, and Abigail felt a bewildering mix of relief and disappointment before giving herself a little shake to clear her head.

The two set off side-by-side.

"I must confess," James said after a moment, "that I have no business to discuss. I just—" he paused. "I wanted to do something nice for you, and I wasn't sure what. You've been so kind to both me and my niece."

"I love her very much," Abigail said earnestly.

James smiled. It didn't quite reach his eyes, but his face was peaceful. "I'm just not certain," he said with a sigh, "when I will stop feeling...."

"Sad?" Abigail suggested a bit timidly, after a few seconds of silence.

"Gutted," James admitted, looking down. The two were shin-deep in daisies now, and when their eyes met, Abigail felt a wave of compassion that cramped her lungs so hard her chest actually hurt. She would have done anything to be able to reach out and touch his cheek the way she would have with one of her brothers, but propriety held her back.

Instead she reached out and gripped his hand in hers, just for a second.

Be a friend.

"You are doing *splendidly*," she said, with all the feeling she could put into the words. "I mean it, James."

"She needs her mother," he said, almost as if he were talking to himself, relaying words he'd said before, alone, without her there. "I don't know if I can—"

"You can and you are," she said firmly, and she squeezed his hand. Hers was absurdly small, almost lost within his, but she repeated it, as if the motion could force what she was trying to say into his head. "You're her family. She needs someone to take care of her and to love her, and you are doing just that. She simply can't have anything better, James."

"Better. Better would be having her parents back." He took a deep, steadying breath, closing his eyes for a moment. When he opened them, they were damp, much as they had been that first night, but his face was more at peace. "But that is impossible. Thank you," he said simply, and he lifted her hand to his lips. "For your kind words."

When his mouth connected with the skin of her hand Abigail felt a thrill that spread lightning-hot from the place, all the way through her body—a flash, then a flush, then a tingle. She *just* managed not to yank her hand back; he squeezed it gently, dropped it, and took a step away from her.

He looked so different there, looking down on her so softly, she thought. He looked younger. Softer. A hint of what she supposed he must have looked like before life and loss had altered him.

"I'm sorry," he said, softly. "Your heart's going like a rabbit's; I felt it in your wrist. Did I frighten you, Abigail?"

"Not at all," she stuttered. "I was—startled, is all. None of my brothers are quite as gallant as you are," she added to lighten the mood a bit, and he smiled.

"Shall we continue our walk, then?"

"Yes, please."

As they walked, enjoying the warm fragrant air of early evening, he talked—about lighter things, this time. Beth's birthday, he said, was coming up in a matter of weeks. "She'll be one. I have no idea what to get her—"

At that, Abigail clapped with glee. "Let's have a party!"

"For a b*aby*?" he said dubiously.

"Oh—she's not a baby, she's a young lady, almost learning to walk and talk! Oh, let's, James. Unless you're still in mourning," she added with some horror. She had not even thought of that. "If that's the case, please forgive me for being so insensitive—"

He shook his head. "No, I'm not interested in subjecting a one-year-old to a year of mourning, Abigail. It is morbid. Your idea is fine—but who in heaven's name will come to a baby's party?"

"Oh, loads of people," she said airily. "There are a few young mothers in town—Elise West, for one, and someone in the Withers family always has a new baby--"

"I don't know any of these people except to do business, Abigail."

"I do. And Mrs. Cross does," Abigail was speaking rapidly, the way she often did when something excited her. "Oh, do let me. It will be so much fun, and a nice way to introduce her to other children in the neighborhood. If she's to live here, you want to do that."

"I suppose so." James looked bewildered. "I suppose you'll handle all the...furbelows?" he asked.

She nodded. "All you have to do is shine your boots and show up as the benevolent host." In her excitement, she skipped and would have met with disaster on a well-placed stone had he not been there to steady her. "Thank you!"

"Hold still, you're making me dizzy," he commanded, but he was smiling.

"I can never hold still when I'm excited," Abigail countered, dancing forward in her high-button boots, "And I love a party. Have you ever hosted anything at the ranch? Does anyone come to call?"

"No one, except for Hiram and Silas and the other hired men, and they are definitely not invited."

"Oh, don't do that! Ask them to send their wives, if they've any young children." Her eyes grew bright. "We can open the house, erect a tent for games, coal-grill steak from your cattle—"

"How much is this going to run me, Abigail?"

Abigail could feel the crestfallen look take over her face, and James laughed aloud when he saw it. "I'm joking, Abigail. Heavens—you look as forlorn as one of my steers, when they get a slap. Do whatever you need to do." He tilted his head, and Abigail was glad to see that the smile reached his eyes, this time. "Your eyes," he said softly, "look remarkably bright."

She brought her hands up to her cheeks; he laughed, reached up and tugged them away, holding them captive in his.

"I'm not certain if I'm going to ever be able to let you go," he said, and the look on his face brought that familiar rush of breath up from her lungs to her throat. "Beth is very lucky to have you."

"She's very lucky to have her uncle," she corrected. He chuckled, and then bent over, and kissed her cheek so quickly she was not even sure it had happened. It should have felt dreadfully improper, but he looked so grateful that somehow, it wasn't. She registered the good clean smell of bay rum and soap, and the faintest scraping of what he would shave off the following morning, and then he was looking down at her again, his eyes the softest she'd ever seen them.

"You're a good girl, Abigail," he said, and his tone was at once so kind, so brotherly, that Abigail suddenly felt as if the enthusiasm had been let out of her like air from a balloon. She took a deep breath; the aftermath of her excitement leaving her feeling slightly dizzy. "I cannot," he said with a laugh, "believe that I've only known you for a week."

"Thank you, James," she said softly.

"Shall we head back, then?"

She nodded. Inexplicably, she suddenly felt very tired.

The days blended into each other with the rapidity that characterizes early fall, and James and his little surrogate household quickly fell into a calm, easy routine. Except for the excitement of a particularly aggressive tooth, little Beth was healthy and strong, and he supposed the mixture of himself, Mrs. Cross, and Abigail, while nowhere near a match for her parents, did very well indeed at keeping the little girl happy.

James found himself relaxing to the point of being able to fully attend to his business. Since Beth had arrived, it had all gone quite a bit topsy-turvy, but knowing she was in Abigail's kind and capable hands allowed for long trips into town now, delivering cattle and beef to clients who had not seen him in weeks.

Perhaps, he thought as he rode into town bright and early on a Monday morning, he could even travel as far as Silverton, and make it a day trip. He could even take Abigail and Beth, if the weather was warm enough. He might treat them to lemonade and stick candy, and visit Silverton's many shops. He could picture Abigail's face brightening at the idea, and he smiled to himself.

It was an unorthodox sort of little family that he'd managed to collect around him, but it was rather wonderful.

James' first stop was at the West Hotel, where Daniel West had been sending telegrams non-stop since James had taken leave to care for Beth. The tall sandy-haired hotelier was there to meet him, squinting out of the back door and waving, a smile on his face.

"Daniel," James said in greeting, stepping down from the wagon and nodding to the two boys that were with his old friend. They scrambled up to the wagon-bed and began unloading the neatly wrapped chunks of beef.

"Welcome back!" Daniel was beaming. "I can't tell you how happy I am to see you—my cook has completely shelved her roasts and beef stews. I think my guests may form a mutiny if I put chicken in front of them, yet again."

James chuckled. He liked the frank, kind hotelier a great deal.

"Won't you come in, James? Have a cool drink, visit a spell."

"That would be nice." the day had been hot and dusty, and James' mouth watered at the thought of cool ginger-water, or a glass of milk.

The two men walked down the dark back hallway, through the bustle in the hotel's enormous kitchen, and into the dining room. Walter Tibbets, the milliner, was there already, drinking from a tall glass of water; James greeted him cordially, expecting that the man had just dropped off flour for Daniel's kitchen.

"Back in action, eh?" Walter said.

"You might say so—oh, thank you," James took an offered glass of sweetened buttermilk from a young woman in a starched white apron, and took a long draw. *Oh.* He peered down at the nutmeg floating on top, impressed. "Most refreshing."

"It's Laura's doing. She's the new cook. Absurdly young, but she conjures something new to serve my guests at least once a week. Elise *loves* her," Daniel said with just enough exasperation to suggest that he was perhaps very happy indeed with their *old* menu. "I'm going to head over and get the ledger from Hannah, James."

"Hannah Cook?" James could not keep any of the five Cook boys straight in his head for any reason, but it was easy enough to remember Hannah, Abigail's older sister, who had walked over to play with Beth a time or two. She looked quite a bit like Abigail, but was taller, with a narrower face and no freckles.

James rather liked freckles.

"Yes—oh, I forget, Abigail is caring for your niece, is she not?"

"She is," James admitted.

"Her sister is absolutely essential to this place. Anyway, give me a moment and I will be back directly."

When he was gone, Walter finished the last drops of his water and put down his glass with a sigh. "I wonder at Cook allowing his daughters to roam about, looking for money so. The oldest," he added, lowering his voice, "was kidnapped on Remembrance Day—some vagrant came to rob the hotel. 'Twasn't an able-bodied man in town who did not help with the search."

"My goodness." James had not been in town for that, although he'd heard about it. "I'm sure they were relieved to have her back safely."

"She shouldn't have been there in the first place," Walter blustered. "Her father barely clears enough on that farm of his to make ends meet. He's looking for threshing work this year in Salem."

"Threshing work?" James was shocked. He knew of many young men that hired themselves out to large farmers in an attempt to earn enough money to buy their own equipment and seed, but for a farmer who'd been at it for two decades and had acres of his own....this was unbelievable. "At his age?"

"Well, what is he going to do? Five great boys and two grown girls, who will likely marry soon..."

James disliked the milliner's gossipy tone, but he indulged it for the sake of conversation. "Indeed?" He wondered suddenly if Abigail had a suitor, and was surprised at how discomfited the thought made him. "The younger looks after my niece."

"Oh, that's right. Very Christian thing you're doing, if unheard of." Walter nodded at James sympathetically. "Many marriages begin on less."

It took James a full moment before he realized what the man was implying. "Sir—"

"Necessary, and—" Walter peered into his face. "Dare I say, she took advantage of a very good opportunity. It is an ideal move, for both of you."

Very good opportunity...? James' heart was pounding strangely. "I'm not sure what you mean."

"Surely, James, you cannot be so naive," Walter chuckled. "Her father is in a dire situation, and you are in a dire situation. Your mutual interests are assured. I've seen her—she's pretty, to boot. Quiet. She will be malleable. You did well."

James was prevented from replying as Daniel reappeared with his ledger and a pen, and Walter quickly became distracted, arguing with Daniel over the price for his flour and bread. James signed his own invoice rather absentmindedly and sat back in his chair, lost in thought.

Your mutual interests are assured....

He pictured Abigail's sweet, gentle face and could not imagine her to be guilty of such cynical goals. Still—her father was in dire straits, and he had a great deal of money, she had been taking care of Beth, who was—for all intents and purposes—his daughter.

Even if Abigail had no designs on him, gossip certainly would not paint it that way. James hated gossip; he hated it more than anything. And now, he felt his face warm as he stared at the back of Walter's ruddy neck. All of a sudden, he saw Abigail's presence in his life through the eyes of the people around them—the slim, petite girl arriving in the morning and leaving at night, the way Beth clung to her and lit up when she arrived, the few times they'd ventured into town on an outing, as if they were a young family.

Even if Abigail was innocent of any deception—and in the deepest part of his heart, he knew she was—Mr. Cook, he thought in a sudden fury, had done nothing to protect his daughter from this type of gossip. In fact, he'd encouraged it. The little voice that had been activated by Walter's blather was growing louder, more insistent—and growing nastier and more insinuating with every word.

Her father dangled a pretty trap in front of you, did he not?

James felt his lungs cramp as air escaped them. He looked up to see Daniel peering at him with some concern.

"Are you all right, man? Your color is bad."

"I am fine." James took a deep breath, trying to steady the beating of his heart. "I wanted to—is your wife available?" he asked after a moment.

"Elise? Why, she's up in our apartments with the baby."

"I'd like to make her a proposal, if I can," James said earnestly. "Beth—my niece. While she is doing splendidly on the farm, I would like her to have the advantage of mixing with other children, which is something I cannot provide her. As your wife is still at home with your boy—would she consider perhaps taking Beth, as well? I would be glad to pay her."

Daniel considered this. "I'd have to ask Elise. She has a mind of her own, but I think she would appreciate the opportunity to earn until she comes back. She sets quite a store in building up her own earnings."

"As she should. There is no reason a woman should be dependent only on her husband's largesse."

"I will ask her. One extra tyke can't make much of a difference, and she has the staff here to help her."

"Thank you, Daniel." The two men shook hands, and James left.

For now, he planned, he would pretend nothing was wrong. Then he'd relieve Abigail of her services as compassionately as he could and send her on her way.

It was the best thing to do, he told himself. Even if she was innocent, even if her father was innocent—it wasn't seemly. His face grew warm at the memory of Walter's smug, sweaty face.

Did everyone think that way? And if James were to be honest with himself, he knew that part of his reaction stemmed from the fact that he knew that he… had an interest in the woman! It was not as though he had taken advantage of Abigail's innocence, nor her sweet nature, but that had not been because he was not attracted to her. Having that acknowledged, having it showcased in such a vulgar way by Walter Tibbets, of all people!—it was downright nauseating.

Swallowing more than a little panic, he climbed up onto the wagon bed, and gave his horse a hearty slap with the reins.

CHAPTER FOUR

*I*t is most fortunate that Beth's birthday has fallen on a Saturday this year, Abigail thought, dancing around James' farmhouse on her toes. She was brimming with excitement. With the help of Mrs. Cross, she had scrubbed every room in the house until the walls and floorboards were bone-white, and picked violets and daisies to stuff into pitchers and bowls, decorating the plain rooms and filling the air with their sweet, heady scent. She had enlisted Hannah's help during the week to cut paper doll chains, snowflakes, and stars, and now they were strung onto every window, sunlight shining through them. She flipped her long braid over her shoulder and exited through the front door, leaving it wide open so the wind and the smell of the sunshine would permeate the house before guests began to arrive.

"Mrs. Cross?" she called.

The older woman was seated on the grass outside, trying with some difficulty to coax Beth into the pink calico dress that had been made for the occasion. "I'm here," she puffed. "How are you, dear?"

"Everything looks wonderful," Abigail said, and she dropped down beside the older woman, her snowy petticoats making a soft crunching sound.

"Who is coming?"

"Well, there's Elise West and her baby, and Rachel Mueller with hers—their children are a few months apart, I believe. Perhaps a year. There's Joanna Taft, and her son, and—"

She finished rattling off her list, and her eyes grew wide. She could see James on the horizon, leading his horse. She leapt up, eliciting a "goodness gracious!" from Mrs. Cross, and ran off in his direction.

"You came!" she said gleefully. James had begged off the occasion, calling it a 'children's party,' and he was probably right, she thought. However, it would have been nice for him as Beth's uncle to at least make an appearance. "Will you stay?"

"I—no. Prancer here's got a stone in his shoe. I'm going to make him comfortable and then head right back out. You said you'd be finished in two hours?"

"Yes, but—" she reached out, grabbing his hand. It was firm and strong as it always was, and a little sweaty from riding. "Do come and see the house," she said enthusiastically. James looked trapped—*typical man,* she thought, but she wasn't going to let him get away with that. "Ten minutes," she promised.

James hesitated, then lifted his shoulders in a sigh. It was hardly an enthusiastic agreement, but Abigail would take what she could get. She scampered off towards the house, James behind her. After a stop to put Prancer in his stall, they headed inside. Abigail raced from room to room, showing him the decorations, the food, chattering on about the games she had planned for their tiny guests. When they finished, standing in the parlor, she let out a breath.

"I hope you do not think me too ridiculous," she said with a laugh. "I'm excited for Beth's birthday. She's a sweet girl and I am eager to give the town a place to welcome and to celebrate her."

James had an odd look on his face; perhaps, Abigail thought

with sympathy, he was thinking of the brother he had lost, and of the mother the little girl should have had. "You mustn't worry about Beth," she said softly. She wanted to reach out and touch his hand—there was something about James, about the cordial aloofness with which he held himself, that made her want to touch him, to comfort him. People who hid their feelings so effectively always needed the most comforting, she found.

"You're a wonderful father," she continued.

His mouth curved up a bit. "I'm not her father, Abigail."

"You are a wonderful uncle, then. The title doesn't matter, really—what matters is that she is safe, and she is loved, and that she has a family. The rest is unimportant."

He tilted his head, looking at her as if he were seeing her for the first time. "You're very wise, Abigail."

She felt color rise into her cheeks. "Not really. I just...well, I have a lot of siblings, and my parents always stressed our family over everything else. You do the same for Beth. You didn't," she added, warming to the subject, "drop her off somewhere and send money for her keep—you brought her home with you, where you would have to deal with her teeth cutting through, and her soiling her linens, and mashing her peas, and her crying—"

"I don't deal with all that, you do," he returned, but his eyes were shining in a way that made his face quite soft and handsome.

"Yes, but it all happens under your roof. And I'm not with you at night, " she returned.

He laughed, and ran his fingers through his hair, not able to quite meet her eyes. "You credit me far more than I deserve, Abigail."

"And you do not credit yourself nearly enough."

Under his sunburn, James' cheeks were flushed, and Abigail was struck suddenly by how absolutely young he looked. They stood, staring at each other for a moment; then James reached behind her and plucked a violet from a white pitcher standing on a side-table. He reached out with both hands and tucked it behind her ear.

The feeling of his warm fingers on the sensitive skin there made her hold back a gasp; the intensity of the feelings he conjured when he touched her was so very unexpected. He lingered there for a moment, rough fingers gentle on the silk of her hair; then, he drew back.

"I'm sorry," he said quietly. "It just looked like it fit."

Abigail's heart was beating strangely, the same way it had been during their walk on Daisy Hill. She had often wondered, after that, if she had imagined the whole thing—not the walk itself, but the sweetness of the moments they had shared. Now, that feeling was back, and she had no idea how to deal with it. James looked—well, almost regretful, and she could not understand why.

She cleared her throat. "Purple is my favorite color," she said, forcing brightness into her voice. She picked up the skirts of her lilac calico—sprigged with purple flowers as it was—it was another hand-me-down from Hannah, and faded from two seasons of laundering, though very well kept.

"It suits you."

"Oh—I haven't even shown you the birthday girl's gift!" Perhaps, Abigail thought, it would get that odd look off his face. She hurried over to the kitchen table. "My brothers made her a wagon from scrap wood—they even painted the wheels yellow. And to ride in it, here's my gift." Abigail opened a box, then held it out for his perusal. In it lay a newly sewn rag doll, her arms extended invitingly. She wore a pink calico dress that had been another donation of Hannah's; her sister had worn it the day she'd been abducted, a year ago. The ruined dress had gone into quilts and aprons, but she'd salvaged enough from the rag-bag to make the doll's dress and sunbonnet. Black yarn had been curled for hair, and red made the rose-bud mouth. Button eyes completed the look. She was gratified to see him chuckle.

"I wrapped up your gift, as well," she said, referring to the collection of bright rubber balls he'd bought the little girl in Silverton.

"She's lucky to have you," he said, and there it was again, that odd look crossing his face. "Abigail—"

They were interrupted when Mrs. Cross came racing into the room, holding Beth at arm's length and scolding frantically. "She's eaten a handful of dirt!"

They both laughed, and the moment was shattered in the chaos.

Beth's party, Abigail thought happily, was better than she had ever imagined it could be.

At exactly one-o-clock, the mothers trailed in one by one, dressed for summer in their thin lawn and calico dresses, in some cases carrying chubby children, in other cases holding them by the hand. Little Beth, fresh from a nap and a meal that Abigail had forced her to take before the festivities began, laughed and clapped and ate everything that was put before her.

As expected James made himself scarce during the festivities, but he did appear when the guests were beginning to collect their things. He made a touching speech about friends, and family, and about the kindness of their tiny community towards his small ward.

"I must also thank Miss Cook," he said, smiling in her direction—a guarded smile, but one that was genuine regardless. "This party is entirely her doing."

He disappeared later, and Abigail put her little charge down for a nap, then began to tidy the house, picking up remnants of food, paper, and decorations. Elise West, who was waiting for her husband to close up for the night and come to bring her home, helped Abigail, and the two young women chatted quietly over a pile of dirty dishes in the kitchen, dunking the plates and glasses in hot soapy water and scrubbing off the remnants of cake, fresh fruit, butter tarts, and lemonade.

"You did well, Abigail," Elise said cheerfully. They could see her son through the open door into the sitting room, where he slumbered peacefully on a blanket. "Oliver and Beth seemed to enjoy each other's company."

"They did."

"I am looking forward to having both of them play together—I think that Oliver grows bored with me." She tossed her hair, and the light gleamed off of the thick, shiny black braids bound at the back of her neck. "What do you plan to do with all your free time?"

"Excuse me?" Abigail was confused.

"Your free time, when you're no longer looking after Beth." Elise tilted her head. "James— he's hired me to look after her, in town, along with Oliver. He seemed to think that you wished to move on to another situation. It's difficult caring for such a young child, but you have done so very admirably."

What?

Abigail stared at Elise, but a yowl from the nursery cut short the conversation.

"I probably should go with you,"so she'll become accustomed to me," Elise whispered. Dumbly, Abigail allowed Elise to follow and the two entered the pale-pink and white freshness of the little room next to James' that was used as a nursery. She watched as Elise deftly plucked the little girl from her bed and soothed her, wiping her tears; then the two women carried Beth back to the kitchen and placed her atop a thick quilt. Beth attempted lunging to her feet, then fell back with a grunt.

"She'll be walking soon, mind my words," Elise said, delighted. "Look at her—she's absolutely determined."

"She pulls herself up on furniture." Even to her, Abigail's voice sounded dull and wooden. "It won't be long."

"She will indeed. My Oliver—"

As the two women talked, Abigail's mind raced wildly. Beth? To be taken care of by Elise? James had obviously decided against having her care for his niece, but—why? What had she done wrong? And why hadn't he told her?

Abigail, if someone had asked her, would not have been able to recount any of the rest of the afternoon's conversation. She chatted pleasantly with Elise until Daniel arrived, kissed the older woman and little Oliver on the cheek, and waved until their buggy disappeared over the horizon. Then she walked back into the house and settled on the floor with Beth, her heart beating strangely in her chest.

James saw the last of the buggies roll away from his home and breathed a sigh of relief. He was mighty hungry, and although he had made his little speech at Mrs. Cross' and Abigail's behest, he'd made a quick retreat after that. He hurried towards the ranch and took a deep breath the moment he stepped inside. He smelled chicken, and some kind of pastry. His stomach growled.

A peek into the kitchen produced Abigail in a large white apron that must have belonged to Mrs. Cross. She was setting his place at the table, while Beth frolicked on a blanket on the floor; the domesticity of the simple scene quite took his breath away.

Abigail looked up as he entered the room, and her small freckled face was sober. "Hello," she said simply. "Mrs. Cross left water for you, if you want to wash up. She went to lie down—I told her I could dish up supper before I left."

"I don't need you to do that, I could easily tend to it myself."

"Mrs. Cross was very concerned that you did not disturb the pastry. It's chicken pie."

He chuckled, but Abigail's expression was still as sober as a judge. He walked over to the basin and pitcher of water, along with a slimy bit of lye soap, and made himself busy washing his face and hands. When he dried them with a snowy towel, he turned; Abigail was burying a spoon deep into the flaky yellow crust, scooping up tender bites of chicken, and bright root vegetables. She spooned piping hot, thin gravy on top, then handed him the plate.

"Won't you have some?" he invited, picking up his fork. Abigail hadn't looked at him once since he'd come inside. It was such a switch from the sunny, exuberant girl he'd met that morning.

She shook her head. "I'm expected at home." She pulled off the filmy apron and folded it; Beth's babbling was the only sound in the room. "I will wait, until you finish your food."

"That's not necessary—I can hold her on my lap. I do that often enough." James held out his arms, and Abigail hesitated for a fraction of a second, then picked the little girl up and handed her to him. James balanced Beth expertly on his knee, then offered her a mashed pea, which she took happily.

"You are very good with her, now," Abigail said softly.

"I like to think so," James said, and he smiled.

"Is that why you're dismissing me?"

The words were so quiet and said with such little emotion that James wasn't quite sure he'd heard them, but the look on Abigail's face completely removed any doubt. He felt the color drain from his cheeks, then rush right back, and he took in a deep breath, rising to his feet so rapidly that Beth squawked. He placed her on the ground at his feet, barely feeling it when she took hold of his trouser leg and tugged herself upwards .

"Abigail—"

"Elise said that you wish to have Beth stay with her during the week." Abigail did meet his eyes then, and he was struck by the guardedness in hers. "Are you...no longer pleased with me?"

"Abigail..."

"I thought...." she checked herself. "So, it's true, then?"

He did not say yes, but he expected that the look on his face was confirmation enough. "Abigail," he began, and licked his lips. "I—do you need the money very much?"

It was the worst possible thing he could have said, and the look on her face made that obvious. "The money?"

"I know your father has fallen on some hard times," James amended, hurriedly, "and you're working to help. If there is anything—if I can help in any way—"

"You just dismissed me!" Her voice had risen, in an octave of utter disbelief and hurt. "Do you intend on making me a charity case, then?"

"No—nothing like that! Abigail, I want to help—"

"Then give me the respect of telling me why you are

dismissing me!" Abigail suddenly looked tall, tall and strong and terrible, her eyes flashing and her full mouth tightening at the corners. She looked very beautiful, he thought almost irrationally, and very, very grown up. Her cheeks were flushed, her hair a golden crown swooping back from her tall forehead, and suddenly the room they were in felt much too small.

He wanted to get up, to take her by the shoulders, to tell her to stop shaking, to take back everything he had said. He wanted to tell her that nothing she had done was wrong, that he was overreacting to vapid, petty gossip, and nothing more. He wanted to tell her that her entry into his life had changed it far beyond what he thought was possible. He wanted to tell her how wrong he was, and that he wanted to take it all back.

Most disturbingly of all, he wanted to kiss her.

James took a step forward, opened his mouth—and Beth, tired of being ignored, let out an indignant squeak. Abigail looked at the baby first—and her face suddenly lit up as brightly as it had been devastated only seconds before.

"James—" she gasped. Her voice cracked. "Look!"

He did. The little girl was standing firmly on two chubby legs, face tight with concentration. She saw Abigail gesture at her and beamed, then toddled two steps forward, straining for her.

"Oh, you clever girl," Abigail breathed out. She looked quite as if she wanted to cry. They both laughed aloud as Beth picked up speed, then immediately crash-landed on her bottom, and began to cry. When James rushed over to her, she pushed him away with both fists and climbed back to her feet.

"She takes to it so easily," James said, not quite able to breathe. The two watched the little girl stagger another few feet; then she fell, and stood again. They clapped for her; she looked startled and clapped for herself, making them both laugh. Then they both seemed to remember what had ensued before Beth had taken her very first steps, and Abigail's face fell again.

"I will go," she said quickly. Beth had toddled over to her and was now clinging to her skirts; it made James curiously sad to see Abigail pry the little girl's hands loose. It seemed cruel to let Abigail go, now that he thought about it. His niece had lost so much already, through no fault of her own.

Abigail crouched down so that she could look the little girl in the eyes; Beth pressed her forehead trustingly to Abigail's, nodded seriously at something she said. Abigail stood; she was blinking rapidly.

"Please pick her up so she won't cry," she whispered.

James went to do so; he felt almost as if he'd murdered someone. "Abigail..."

"I will go," she said, and headed to the door. In an instant, she was outside, her slender form flashing past the window. She was running in the direction of the Cook family farm, leaving the smell of chicken pie and violets in her wake, and a crying toddler in James' arms.

It was actually several hours before she made it home that night.

One hour was reserved for having a good cry, in the shadow of a grove of trees that separated her father's property from James' ranch. She could hear the bellowing of the cattle a short distance away, and the howls of the sheep-dogs that would run at their heels until they were safely locked in their pens for the night. Work on the ranch would continue without her. The animals would sleep, and inside, Mrs. Cross would ready little Beth for bed, tuck her into her small white crib, and whisper a prayer to her before she slept. James would wash and have a cup of creamy coffee and look over his ledger before climbing into bed himself. She was not needed for any of it, and she would not be there for any of it ever again.

She would miss Beth. Abigail had formed a real attachment to the little girl over the weeks she'd taken care of her, and was as proud of her growth and health as if she were her own mother. However, it was not the thought of Beth that had her crying now—it's was James, and the look in his eyes as he'd dismissed her. He had humiliated her. *Rejected* her.

He made her feel, if only a moment, as useless as she had before she'd taken on the job of nanny. More so.

I know your father has fallen on some hard times…

If so, then what? What did that have to do with her, and her relationship with Beth? He'd looked so flushed and uncomfortable, and then he'd offered her help, offered her *charity*—

She squeezed her eyes shut at the memory. Anger was rapidly fading, replacing itself with an acute hurt that manifested as a dull ache, somewhere beneath her ribs. She rubbed frantically at her face with her skirt; she could not go home now. Her face swelled so abominably when she cried.

She lay on her belly in the grass, breathing in the sweet, earthy smell beneath the summer sky and refused to acknowledge the trickle of hot tears that would not stop. The warmth was soothing. Soon the sun would be down, and she would have to return to the house and face her brothers, acting as if nothing was wrong. For now, she told herself, she would rest, and try not to think about what had just happened.

Abigail returned home after a thorough washing of her face in the brook, and after she'd brushed the grass off her skirts. Luckily her mother was rolling pastry for Sunday morning apple turnovers and her brothers were doing the evening chores; the only one she encountered before fleeing to her room was Hannah, who was frowning down at a basket of mending in her mother's easy-chair.

"How was the party?" she called to her younger sister.

"Oh, it was fine," Abigail said, trying to speak carelessly. "I'm going up to change." She ran rapidly up the stairs and mounted the ladder to their attic bedroom, her heart pounding. She stripped off her dress, shoved it into the crate they used for soiled clothing, and climbed into she and Hannah's big bed. She didn't even bother to loose her stays.

When her older sister came in, she was laying in the dark on a very damp pillow.

"Abigail?" she whispered.

Abigail did not make a sound; perhaps her sister would think her asleep.

"You never showed for dinner. Mama thought perhaps you were so tired you slept off." She heard the soft plink of silverware being set down on a china plate. "I've brought you some ginger-bread, and a glass of milk." There was another pause, and Hannah spoke again, very gently this time. "I know you're not asleep, Abigail. You snore dreadfully."

At that, Abigail sat up indignantly, and her sister chuckled. "I thought you were up."

"Don't light the lamp!" Abigail said quickly, swiping furtively at her cheeks in the dark. "Just a candle is fine, Hannah. Thank you. I—I was very close to drifting off," she added.

There was the striking of a match, and her sister's concerned face appeared in a circle of wavery light. Abigail threw off the covers and put her feet on the floor, falling eagerly on the spicy gingerbread and warm milk. She was hungry, she discovered after the first couple of bites.

Hannah walked to the window and opened it. The warmth of the day had risen, making their little room stiflingly hot most nights; in her miserable state, Abigail had not even noticed it, but now she felt sticky and uncomfortable. She began to wriggle about, trying to loosen her stays.

"No—eat. I'll do it." Hannah came over, and Abigail was comforted by her sister's soft hands and the smell of rose water that hung round her like a soft fragrant mantle. She sighed as she was able to finally draw a deep breath, and felt her sister's small chin rest on her shoulder.

"How was the party?" she asked again.

"It was lovely." This Abigail could say with no hesitation, at least. "The children had a wonderful time—and, oh, Beth took her first steps!" she remembered. There was joy in that awful day, after all.

"Did she like the dolly?"

"Yes, but she liked the wagon more. We couldn't persuade her out of it."

"And James Taylor?"

"He was absent for most of the festivities, but came at the end to thank everyone who came." Abigail was proud that her voice did not tremble when she spoke of James, but there must have been something there, for her sister grew quiet, and then she said—

"Are you all right, Abigail?"

Abigail considered lying, then realized she didn't really want to. "No," she admitted. "But I will be." Normally she would have poured everything out to Hannah right in that moment, but something held her back. James wasn't merely a school-boy who had offended her, or a friend she was feeling peevish about. This was something so much deeper, and she wanted to keep it to herself for now, to think quietly about it.

Hannah hesitated. "Has James Taylor been—a gentleman?"

It took Abigail a moment to understand her sister's meaning; then, she was grateful for the darkness that hid her blush. "He has been without reproach, in that area," she said after a moment, tucking her hands beneath her arms.

"Good," was all Hannah said, and she leaned forward to kiss the top of Abigail's head. "I am going to undress, and climb in bed," she announced. "Rinse the plates in the wash-basin, and we can take them down in the morning."

"Thank you, Hannah."

Her sister's hands were at her hair now, carefully undoing the heavy braid that lay on the back of her neck, combing through her long locks with nimble fingers. "You've something here," she said, and handed Abigail the violet that James had tucked behind her ear with such gentleness, only that morning. She swallowed hard.

"We used them as decorations," she explained, and she crushed the little bud cruelly in her fist. Its heady perfume still wafted up to her nose, and she quickly wiped her hand on the damp towel her sister had included with her meal.

Later, when Hannah was curled beside her, breathing softly

in sleep, Abigail lay on her back, staring up at the ceiling, and thought—hard. She still did not know why James had discarded her so decidedly, or understand the pain she knew she'd seen in his eyes when she'd showed him how devastated she was. All she knew for sure was that she would miss Beth, and that despite being furious with James, she would miss him. Very much.

Her mind swirled about for another few minutes. Outside the open window, her eyes found the stars, and she sighed as she listened to the crickets in the front garden proclaim their love for them.

Then she rolled over and closed her eyes. Tomorrow was a new day.

CHAPTER FIVE

Although she had fallen asleep late and slept badly, Abigail was up before the sun, at the same time as Hannah. She asked her sister determinedly if she could go into town with her.

Hannah looked surprised. "Are you not headed to the Taylor farm anymore, Abigail?"

She shook her head. "James Taylor no longer requires my services," she said, and now that she had managed to get it out, she felt much better. Her insides still felt battered, but that would dissipate with time. "I would like to look for another situation."

"Heavens, where?"

"Mrs. Brown is always looking for girls."

"Cleaning, Abigail? In a boarding-house?" Her sister's voice rose an octave in surprise. "That sort of work—"

"There is no reason I cannot do that sort of work," she said, a little bitterly. "This entire family has coddled me for years, Hannah, and I have rather enjoyed it. I need to grow up," she added, half to herself. In her long, restless night, she'd come to that realization. Nothing was guaranteed—not a friendship, not a job, not a relationship, but you had to learn from your mistakes, move on, and do better.

Hannah looked surprised, but said little apart from— "I leave in an hour, dearest."

The two clattered down the stairs together, hand-in-hand. When they dressed to go into town Abigail took her long braid, wound it round her head, and pinned it firmly in place. Her sister smiled.

"Putting your hair up?"

"It should be up," Abigail admitted. "I'm nineteen. If people want to take me seriously, I should take myself seriously." She sped through her chores with mounting excitement, and packed a pail lunch of cold potatoes and cornbread spread with honey—her family's hives had produced that year, though the fields had not. Hannah would likely eat at the hotel. She stood impatiently waiting for her older sister, and they ambled into town side by side.

Abigail realized very quickly that she had no idea how to go about finding work; when she said this to her older sister, Hannah laughed kindly. "Why not spend the morning with me?" she said. "Many merchants from town come through the hotel on business, and we can ask there, instead of you traipsing about to them. When we lunch we can go to see Mrs. Green, too—she hasn't been able to replace Marylee since she got engaged to Dr. Lavan, and is still in nursing school."

"I should think that Marylee would prefer working for Mrs. Green," murmured Abigail. She could not picture her sunny, fun-loving old classmate enamored with the town's sardonic doctor, but there was no accounting for taste. "And I'm a dreadful seamstress, you know this."

"You do well with finishing. Seams and buttons and hems and such."

"That is true..." Abigail's shoulders sagged a little at the thought of all that work she hated, but there was no getting round it. Sewing was likely to be the only job she would find, and if she did not want to leave disappointed, it was best she accept it.

Once they arrived at the hotel and Hannah was settled behind the front desk, Abigail amused herself by wandering around a bit, then decided to go up to Elise and Daniel's apartments to say hello. She wondered with a pang if Beth would be there, and if she would be able to take it if she were.

Beth was not there, and Abigail learned through some very subtle questioning that the little girl was traveling with her uncle and Mrs. Cross to Silverton—"to buy her a pony, now that she's walking," Elise said in disbelief. In spite of her pain, Abigail had to chuckle—it sounded so like James to do that.

"He's a doting uncle."

"Indeed he is." Elise looked at her keenly. "Was it your idea to stop minding Beth?"

"It was a mutual agreement." Abigail was mentally prepared for this line of questioning, and so she answered stoutly.

"You did very well with the party," Elise said after a moment. "have you ever thought of teaching, Abigail?"

At that Abigail was surprised; she had not expected the conversation to veer in that direction. "Teaching?"

"Yes. You are cheerful, empathetic and energetic. I think you have the ideal qualities of a teacher."

"I..." Abigail had simply never thought of it; she was barely three years out of the school-room, herself. She thought hard for a moment; then, she shook her head. "I don't think so. I enjoy children in the nursery, but I wouldn't know what to do with older ones."

Elise smiled. "Think about it."

"I will."

Oliver was racing around the room, spinning gleefully till he fell on his seat; both woman laughed. "Oliver," Abigail called, "Will you sit with me, perhaps? Come here, dear, and I'll show you how to make a paper hat..."

Suddenly, inexplicably, in the face of this little boy's joy, Abigail felt incredibly peaceful.

It would all be fine; she was sure of it.

James faced down three restless, uncomfortable nights before admitting that guilt was keeping him awake.

It gnawed at him during the day, when he watched Beth, and how subdued she was with Mrs. Cross, and how her large eyes often wandered to the door, as if she were expecting someone who hadn't yet shown. He felt guilty whenever he saw the little rag doll and wagon that Abigail had so thoughtfully given Beth, and the guiltiest of all when he caught sight of Mr. Cook's fields laying fallow in the early-autumn sun. This had been a hopeless entanglement, really; he should have known it would have been a terrible idea, from the beginning. But Abigail had been so sweet, and Beth had gravitated towards her like a moth to warm flame. He realized now that's what was it—he could not deny the little girl anything, not after the extent of what had been lost already. Who knew what damage he was doing to her tiny mind?

James was forced to think about himself, as well, and what he wanted. He was twenty-three, and until recently; he'd had no thought of marriage, or anything like, but Abigail's gentle voice and sweet face seemed to invade his thoughts at the oddest moments these days. It was on this third day, when he was alone with his cattle and his thoughts, that he dared to ask himself the question that had been echoing in his heart's mind since Abigail had left him alone in the kitchen, with little but the memory of that crushed look on her face.

His arrogance, in retrospect, shamed him. He, listening to idle gossip—!

His older brother, he thought, would be ashamed of him. Caleb never hesitated to do what was right, even if the consequences were unpalatable. As a young homesteader, James had been fighting for the respect of his peers since he'd purchased his first acre, but as a human being? He was afraid, when he examined himself deep down inside, that he'd failed both Abigail and himself rather miserably.

He stood for a long moment, chewing his lip and looking out over the waving grasses of the plain; then, he dragged his hat off his head, reluctantly, and wiped his forehead. He began to walk, his boots barely making a sound; as he did, he thought harder.

Was it, he wondered, so bad, the idea of his courting a girl—this girl? Had Abigail's appearance on his doorstep just as he needed her been Providential, and not deliberate? Was anything else except his pride and stubbornness standing in the way of exploring a possibility that might make both of them happy? Besides—

She is innocent in this.

Another wave of shame took James, and he took a deep, painful breath.

He knew exactly what he had to do.

James found Abigail's father out on the southern part of his land, amid furrows of what should have been shocks of oats. He was crouched in a freshly plowed furrow, squeezing damp dirt in his hand. When James came upon him, he spoke without looking up.

"You'll not find my daughter here, Mr. Taylor," the man said, slowly.

James felt his cheeks burn. "I'm not looking for Ab—for Miss Cook, sir."

Mr. Cook straightened and stood to his feet. Abigail looked a great deal like him—he was slight and freckled as well, although his face was mostly covered by a grey-streaked beard, and deep-set eyes that probably would have been humorous, in a different setting. "Can I help you, son?"

James took a deep breath. I have a proposition for you, sir."

"Aside from hiring my daughter, you mean?"

His stomach tightened. "You were amiable."

"Yes, and so were you, until last week." The man's laconic tone threatened to become razor-sharp at any moment.

"Sir—" James felt his mouth dry up.

"Why are you here, Mr. Taylor?"

James took a deep breath. "I don't know what Abigail told you—"

"She didn't have to tell me anything. I've seen her face for the past couple of days, and now I'm seeing yours, and I'm not sure you want me to reach a conclusion without context."

James' face felt like it was being baked on coals. He was silent for a moment—he didn't want to bungle this as badly, as he had done with Abigail.

"I owe her," he said quietly, "an apology. Not for anything you need to worry about, sir," he added hurriedly. "But an apology, nonetheless."

"Whenever one of my children is upset, I'm worried," he said tartly, but James could see a subtle but definite change in the man's expression; he had relaxed.

"I understand, sir." He hesitated, then forged on. "I would—like to come see her, with your permission."

The older man's eyes narrowed. "To beg her pardon?"

"Why—yes, of course. But after—" James cleared his throat, and Mr. Cook's mouth twitched, once.

"How old are you?"

James was startled at the question, but he recovered gamely. "I am twenty-three, sir."

"You look older."

"I've been doing a man's job for some time."

"Clearly. Your parents?"

"Dead, sir."

"I wondered. It's very unusual for a young man to take on the care of a baby."

"She has no one else, sir." James hesitated, then spoke again. "And until a few days ago, she had Abigail. I'd like to remedy that, sir. I took something very important away from her."

Mr. Cook grunted. "I will be frank, young James. I fear that your desire to—visit my daughter is tied mainly to her care of your ward."

Shame burned deep in the pit of James' stomach. Here he'd

been focusing selfishly on his own suspicions, while Mr. Cook had some of his own. When he spoke, it was quiet, and low.

"It was Beth that brought us together, sir," he said. For the first time in their conversation, the words were coming as easily as wheat being poured from a sack; kernels of truth were sliding out with smooth rapidity. "I will forever be grateful to her for that, even though she will have no idea why. And if my brother came back to life today and came to collect my niece, I would still ask leave to court your daughter."

There. He'd said it. The two men looked at each other for a long moment; then, Mr. Cook extended a hand.

"I thought you arrogant," he said, simply.

"I was."

"Yes, well."

James took a deep breath. "Sir? If I might, I have another proposal for you."

The older man raised his brows.

When the idea came to Abigail, it did with startling clarity, astonishing her so much that she actually froze in the middle of the path while carrying a pail of water in for her mother. She placed it down carefully, washed her hands, then told her mother with astonishing calm that she was going into town.

"What, at this hour, Abigail?" her mother frowned. Abigail had taken two days to look for work, with no luck whatsoever, although she was still optimistic.

"Yes, Mama. Please. I'd like to see Elise West."

"Whatever for?" Mrs. Cook was stirring a pot of cornmeal-mush, doing the painstaking job of sprinkling cornmeal, pinch by pinch, into a bubbling pot. Had Abigail been making it, the mush certainly would have turned into a lumpy mess.

"I have an idea I'd like to discuss with her."

Mrs. Cook sighed. "Abigail—"

"Please, Mama."

"It is fine. You may go. But—perhaps, Abigail, you should become a little bit—realistic about your future. Working on your father's farm is not the end of the world."

"I love you, Mama." She kissed her mother's cheek and scampered for the door.

Bolstered by her excitement, Abigail ran all the way to town, into the West Hotel, and took the stairs up two by two to the West apartment. When she knocked, and Elise opened; she exclaimed.

"Why, Abigail!"

Abigail was a sight, indeed; she was red-faced, rather sweaty, and her hair had come loose and was hanging over one shoulder. "You look like a wild woman, child. Are you all right? No—no, don't try to speak. Come in and have some water."

When Abigail entered the bright, pleasant room, she laughed, for Beth was there, and she ran for Abigail on sturdy little legs, clearly having been practicing her steps with determined energy. Abigail picked up the little girl, kissing her on both cheeks, her forehead, her little button-nose. When she surfaced for air Elise was smiling indulgently.

"Elise," she said, now that she could speak. "Let's start a school!"

Abigail fairly danced home hours later, in the purple-gold twilight, her eyes just as bright as the sky at dusk. She was so happy her face was absolutely transformed; her mother started when she burst into the kitchen.

"Oh—Mama, I've had the most wonderful idea!" she cried. "Elise and I are opening a nursery!"

"I—what?"

"We will watch young children at the West Hotel for a fee, and I will be in charge!" Abigail was pacing, excitedly. "Many women with young children come to the hotel without their maids—it's an added expense. There also may be some young mothers who would like an hour or two to themselves to shop, or run errands—" she took a deep breath. "I realized I could do it when I planned Beth's party. I met near every young woman in town, then. They all agreed that it is difficult, being shut in with a little one all day."

"Will women be willing to pay for this, Abigail?"

"We will make it affordable, mother, and they only need to pay for the time they need. Also, Elise suggested we offer bartering—take goods as well as money. The hotel guests will be charged more as they will have more money to spend, so it will all even out in the end."

Her mother's dark brows raised to the limit. "Very interesting idea."

"I will have my own business—well, part of a business." Abigail very nearly skipped, but she forced herself to calm down. "Mama? What do you think?"

Her mother's face creased into a smile. "I am quite proud of your creativity, darling. I think it is a splendid idea."

Abigail kissed her mother's cheek again, then pressed hers to the older woman's face. She felt happier than she had in days— and this way, she would be able to see Beth as well. Everything was better again. Well—nearly everything.

She missed James. And she supposed that would not go away, not for quite some time.

"Abigail?" her mother's soft voice broke into her thoughts. She opened her eyes and looked at her.

"I am very, very proud of you."

"Thank you, mother," she said, softly.

Her mother went back to her pot of cornmeal, stirring briskly. "Now," she said, "While you were in town, your James Taylor came to see your father."

Your James... Abigail started so violently that she bumped against the table, and stirring-cups clattered to the floor. Her mother cried out.

"Lands alive!"

"What did he...what did he want, Mama?" Abigail burst out, picking up the cups with trembling fingers.

"It's actually quite extraordinary." Her mother looked to see that her daughter had succeeded in clearing up, then went back to her brisk stirring, moving the food to a cooler area of the stove so that it would cook slowly. "He wishes to lease your father's land, have him erect temporary lean-tos on several acres. Apparently he had quite a windfall when it came to crops this year, and he wishes to use our land for storage, now that it will lay fallow until next year."

Abigail was speechless.

"He is giving your father a very generous amount for the use of his land," her mother added almost casually, then she turned to look her youngest daughter in the eye. "More than enough for your father to replenish his seed for next year, and plenty left over to see us through the winter." She turned her back on her daughter, opened the pantry, and began to rummage, taking down a bottle of dark molasses.

"He asked," her mother finally added, "if he could call on you. Formally."

At that, Abigail's head snapped up. Her mother continued with her breakfast preparations as if nothing had happened, and after two wild minutes of Abigail staring at her mother, she turned wordlessly and banged her way out of the kitchen. That caught her mother's attention.

"Abigail Jane Cook—*Abigail!* Where are you—? Oh no, off she goes again, in her house dress and everything, with her hair streaming in the wind like a crazy woman. *Abigail!*"

As she'd done that morning, Abigail cut the time it took to make it to James' farm nearly in half. She tore past a very confused Mrs. Cross, who was tending to the vegetable garden, and burst into the house, shouting his name. She knew that he was there—she'd seen his horse still tied in the front of the house. She looked into the parlor, into Beth's room, and finally burst into the kitchen—and stopped short.

James was standing there, suspenders hanging down, naked to the waist. A basin of steaming water stood in front of him; his skin was damp. Abigail gave a little shriek and whirled round, covering her face.

"Why are you—?!"

"Why am *I?*" She could heard rustling as James—hopefully—pulled on his shirt. "You're the one who burst in here, shouting like a cowboy!"

They stood in silence for a moment; Abigail heard water being poured.

"Can I turn around now?" she said after a moment, almost meekly.

"That's up to you."

Abigail scowled and turned herself about. James was staring at her, his eyes soft, his hair darkened by the water and lying flat against his head. She kept her gaze firmly above his shoulders. His lean musculature was nothing like that of her brothers, and the linen of his shirt was clinging to his shoulders and torso in the most distracting way.

His lips tipped up, ever so slightly. "You're red."

"I ran all the way here." She took a deep breath, desperately grasping for the fury that had sustained her journey. James took a step towards her; she felt her heart began thudding dully in her chest.

"I owe you an apology," he said, gently. "I wanted to make it with flowers in hand in your mother's parlor, but you ruined my plan."

Abigail closed her eyes. *No!* She did not want to relent so easily, despite his charm. She could hear him, moving closer to her.

"Abigail," he said. "I am sorry."

"I am not sure you quite understand what you're apologizing for," she said, and oh—*horrors!* Her voice was beginning to tremble, just a little.

"I certainly do, and I regret hurting you very much." He took a deep breath. "I was foolish and arrogant, Abigail. I did it because—well. I like you. People saw it, and they said things, and I panicked. You are—good, and kind, and absolutely perfect. And I wish to do what I should have done before."

Abigail crossed her arms over her chest, protectively. "Which is?"

"Ask to see you. Properly." He hesitated. "I'm sorry, Abigail, that I'm bungling this so badly. I never have done this before."

At that, Abigail felt her cheeks flush further still. "Neither have I."

The two stood in silence for a moment, staring at each other; then, Abigail cleared her throat.

"What happens now?" she said quietly.

James smiled. "I suppose—I shall come to see you. I'll pick flowers along the way, perhaps bring you a box of horehound candy—"

"Chocolate drops," Abigail interrupted.

James grinned. "—Chocolate drops, and we'll sit in your Mama's parlor. We'll talk. Possibly flirt, but not too much as to make it improper. I might kiss you, if you'll let me. And then—" he lifted his shoulders. "I know what I would like to happen, but I do not want to make any assumptions about you. For now, I only want your —permission to do that much." He paused, cleared his throat. "Your eyes are shining."

Abigail's heart was beating so hard that she was sure that he could hear it. He was standing there, unkempt and handsome—his hair lit from the light of the window behind him—looking very much like the hero on a the cover of dime store novel.

What else could she say? She could hardly tell him that this was the one thing she'd never dared to hope for, or that she'd been dreaming of the things he spoke of for weeks now.

"You have my permission," she said softly.

James' responding grin was hazy with the light from the setting sun.

EPILOGUE

I *f tongues had wagged over* James' initial employment of Abigail, they were sent into a veritable frenzy at their marriage. Less than six months after James began visiting the Cook household with regularity, the couple married at the West Hotel. Flanked by her siblings and rosy from all of their kisses, Abigail was swung up into a brand-new buggy with her skirts streaming, and she accepted little Beth into her arms with a loving smile. She rearranged her striped pale silk—her first silk dress! —and rode off towards the Taylor Ranch beside her new husband, tossing a bouquet of violets out behind her as they went.

Her father had been a firm advocate of the marriage. "Start your life early; it's for the best," he declared when he gave his blessing.

In true farming fashion, they put off a honeymoon until the end of the planting season, and instead of a wedding present, her six brothers erected a child-sized cottage on the property for Beth to play in. There was another one, too, at the West Hotel, where Abigail and Elise's growing brood of nursery-students frolicked each week.

Now, two weeks later, the couple sat together on the front lawn, feasting on a cold lunch of bread, butter, honey and a beautifully roasted chicken.

"Beth!" Abigail called across the yard; and the little girl, where she was attempting to stuff a fistful of grass into her mouth, was distracted. She stood carefully and toddled over to where Abigail and James lounged in the grass. James looked around lazily, and smiled as Beth came near.

"Howdy, sweet girl."

"She has something to tell you," Abigail said, dimpling hard. James sat up immediately, and at Abigail's prompting, Beth scooted shly over to him, placing her fat hands on his knee.

"Love. Papa," she said clearly, then she ran off again.

James was left with his mouth hanging wide open; those two words were as plain as day. He turned to his wife, who clapped her hands joyfully.

"I coached her," she bubbled. "She's brilliant, isn't she?"

"You both are," James said with all the conviction of the young and newly married; and he closed the distance between he and his wife, kissing her soundly. She squealed in protest, but only half-hardheartedly.

"James—Mrs. Cross—!"

"She's been married before. She knows to make herself scarce," he said roughly.

Abigail giggled and tried to escape, but her husband was too fast, if not too dexterous. His hands closed around her waist just as they both lost their balance. The picnic did not escape; Abigail felt what must have been quite a bit of bread, smooshing under her left arm. She didn't care, though; she squeezed her eyes shut, and kissed her husband so hard she saw stars.

In that very moment, Abigail knew that happiness had found her. It had blessed her with a dear husband and a daughter, and wrapped its arms around her, and she was *never* going to let it go. As little Beth giggled, and toppled onto the picnic blanket beside them, and the couple broke apart laughing, she understood the absolute truth... that their love, and their little family—from that moment onward—would only grow.

The End

Take a Step Back into Adoration
with
BRENDEN'S BOOKISH BRIDE
Book Three in the *Matchmaker's Mix Up* Series
AND
A Special *Brides of Adoration* Story

Patient and quiet, **Margarette Bates** is accustomed to hard work. Her only distraction from the grim realities of the New York workhouses are the novels she has grown to love. When a chance comes for her own romantic escape to the wilds of Adoration, Oregon, she takes it without hesitation—only to find that her romantic hero-to-be is actually a perpetually irritated man well into middle age.

Horrified at their matchmaker's inexcusable mix-up, the two quickly strike a bargain—she'll work as his housekeeper, and leave as soon as she can find another situation. However, love is determined to find Margarette within the city limits of Adoration, and if not with her new employer, might it be in the arms of his handsome son?

Henry Weller always intended to see to his father's happiness before his own, but when Margarette Bates arrives in Adoration...his resolve is put to an unexpected test. As his father's affection for the woman grows into something more serious, Henry must choose between a passion he never thought possible and the love of his own flesh and blood.

Can the bride that he intended for his father truly be meant for him?

● · ○ · ● · ○ · ● · ○ · ● · ○ · ●

BRENDEN'S BOOKISH BRIDE

is the third book in the AMAZING *Matchmaker's Mix-Up*
Series, it is also a *Brides of Adoration* story. This is a tale of clean,
old-fashioned romance, free of cliff-hangers and profanity,
with a happily ever after that will warm your heart.

Grab the next release from *#1 Bestselling Author,* Josephine
Blake, by going to Amazon.com and searching for
Brenden's Bookish Bride!!

ABOUT THE AUTHOR

Josephine Blake is a bestselling author and award-winning graphic designer. She enjoys a quiet life on a comfortable piece of property in her very own small-town in the Willamette Valley.
With many published books in the romance genre, Josephine works hard to make sure her stories bring a little more love into this crazy world.
She and her husband spend most days chasing their little one around their farmhouse with thankful hearts.

Notable Works:
Josephine Blake's debut Historical Romance novel, *Dianna*, hit the shelves in August of 2016 and became a bestseller two years later. Her Gothic Historical Romance novel, *A Brush with Death*, followed suit later that year in 2018. *Yours at Yuletide* became her very first Contemporary Romance Bestseller in the winter of 2019.

She'd love to hear from you. Shoot her an email at **admin@awordfromjosephineblake.com.**

HAPPY READING!

Made in the USA
Middletown, DE
26 November 2020